学术顾问

（以姓氏笔画为序）

王　宏　冯智文　李正栓　李丽生　原一川

Academic Advisors

Wang Hong　Feng Zhiwen　Li Zhengshuan

Li Lisheng　Yuan Yichuan

主　编

李昌银

副主编

黄　瑛　彭庆华

General Editor

Li Changyin

Professor of English Yunnan Normal University

Associate General Editors

Huang Ying

Professor of English Yunnan Normal University

Peng Qinghua

Professor of English Yunnan Normal University

云南少数民族经典作品英译文库

Classics of Yunnan Ethnic Groups in English Translation

主编 李昌银　General Editor　Li Changyin
副主编 黄瑛 彭庆华　Associate General Editors　Huang Ying & Peng Qinghua

Zhisa Jiabu
支萨·甲布

演唱◎独几品初
　　　阿格光布等
搜集整理◎殷海涛　杨增烈
英译◎刘德周
译校◎[美]包琼

Sung by Dujipinchu, Ageguangbu et al
Collected & Edited by Yin Haitao & Yang Zenglie
Translated by Liu Dezhou
Revised by Joan Cecile Boulerice

云南出版集团
云南人民出版社

图书在版编目（CIP）数据

支萨·甲布：汉、英/独几品初等演唱；殷海涛，杨增烈搜集整理；刘德周英译. -- 昆明：云南人民出版社，2018.12

（云南少数民族经典作品英译文库/李昌银主编）

ISBN 978-7-222-17506-8

Ⅰ. ①支… Ⅱ. ①独… ②殷… ③杨… ④刘… Ⅲ. ①普米族—民间故事—中国—汉、英 Ⅳ. ①I277.3

中国版本图书馆CIP数据核字(2018)第277404号

出 品 人	李　维	赵石定
项目统筹	周　祥	殷筱钊
项目组稿	郭木玉	
责任编辑	郭木玉	任建红　李东华
设计制作	马　滨	三人禾
责任校对	张齐英	崔苡菡　付芳侠　周桉吉
责任印制	陆卫华	代隆参

云南少数民族经典作品英译文库
Classics of Yunnan Ethnic Groups in English Translation

支萨·甲布
Zhisa Jiabu

演唱◎独几品初　阿格光布等
搜集整理◎殷海涛　杨增烈
英译◎刘德周
译校◎[美]包琼

Sung by Dujipinchu, Ageguangbu et al
Collected & Edited by Yin Haitao & Yang Zenglie
Translated by Liu Dezhou
Revised by Joan Cecile Boulerice

出　版	云南出版集团　云南人民出版社
发　行	云南人民出版社
社　址	昆明市环城西路609号
邮　编	650034
网　址	www.ynpph.com.cn
E-mail	ynrms@sina.com
开　本	787mm×1092mm　1/16
印　张	6.5
字　数	100千
版　次	2018年12月第1版第1次印刷
印　刷	云南出版印刷（集团）有限责任公司　云南新华印刷一厂
书　号	ISBN 978-7-222-17506-8
定　价	39.00元

云南人民出版社
公众微信号

序 一

◎李正栓

民族典籍英译是传播中国文化、文学和文明的重要途径，是中华文化走出去的重要组成部分。文化与文学的传播，是一个国家提高文化软实力的重要方式，在文化交流和文明建设中起着不可或缺的作用，对提高国家对外话语权、构建国家对外话语体系以及对建设世界文学都有积极意义。

中国各少数民族拥有许多优秀的典籍，具有很高的文物价值、文学价值和文化价值。各民族的先人们通过口头流传或用文字记述了他们各具特色的文化。各少数民族几乎都有自己民族的创世史、史诗和神话传说。

中国民族典籍独具特色，不可替代。重视民族典籍的翻译和研究工作，对于挖掘各民族优秀文化，保护各民族文明，增强各民族之间的沟通和了解，进一步向世界其他地区传播各少数民族优秀文化，乃至提高我国文化软实力都有着重要意义。不少少数民族聚居地处于祖国边疆，有的处在"一带一路"建设关键部位，有的处在与周边国家进行各种交流的重要位置。

中国民族典籍是世界多元文化的有机组成部分，与其他文化共同造就了世界文化的绚丽多姿。世界正因为其文化多样性才变得缤纷多彩。我国各民族典籍中包含的文化多样性极大地丰富了世界多元、特色鲜明的文化。人们对多样性形成全新的认识角度和思维方式。多样性开阔了人们的视野，丰富了人们思考问题的角度。挖掘这些典籍中所蕴含的教育价值和文化价值，对世界其他民族都有指导和借鉴意义，并且有助于建设我国的文化自信。

民族典籍本身蕴含的特殊价值对加强民族文化了解、促进中外文化交流具有重大意义。民族典籍英译具有文学翻译和文化传递之功能，有对外宣传作用，还是一种文学外交。因此，民族典籍翻译和研究对于维护祖国统一、促进民族团结、稳定边疆以及增强国内各民族和中外文化之间的交流都起着极为重要的作用。

中华人民共和国成立以后，中央政府一直十分重视民族典籍翻译和研究工作，提供了强有力的政策支持，并采取了一系列有效措施，加快了各少数民族典籍的抢救、整理、翻译和研究的进程。中央政府多次召开西藏工作会议和新疆工作会议。近年来，国际和国内对于多元文化高度关注，少数民族文学典籍的翻译已然成为业内研究的热点。

近年来，民族典籍翻译和研究迅猛发展，势头良好。国家大力支持，发放国家社科基金课题，教育部和国家民委也发放课题，扶持了一大批研究者。很多民族典籍翻译课题得以立项并顺利开展；为数不少的民族典籍被翻译成汉语、英语和其他语言并出版发行；越来越多的业界人士致力于这个满富生机的学术领域。

在中国文化走出去的国家战略下，全国少数民族典籍英译学术研讨会陆续召开，已经召开三次。

云南是中国民族最多的省份。人口在5000人以上的少数民族有25个，其中有15个民族为云南所特有，分别是：白族、哈尼族、傣族、傈僳族、佤族、拉祜族、纳西族、景颇族、布朗族、普米族、阿昌族、基诺族、怒族、德昂族、独龙族。其中除白族人口占全国白族人口总数的84%以上外，其他14个民族95%居住在云南。

云南还是我国跨境民族最多的省份。在云南的25个少数民族中，有16个民族跨境而居，分别是：傣族、壮族、苗族、景颇族、瑶族、哈尼族、德昂族、佤族、拉祜族、彝族、阿昌族、傈僳族、布依族、怒族、布朗族、独龙族。

云南少数民族创造了辉煌的文化。据不完全统计，云南少数民族文字文献古籍蕴藏量达10万余册（卷），口传古籍4万余种。云南省民委少数民族古籍整理出版规划办公室为了挽救和保护这些古籍，计划在5年内编纂出版100卷《云南少数民族古籍珍本集成》。这是一个令人瞩目的庞大计划。将这些古籍中的珍品翻译介绍给世界，不仅能够弘扬云南省丰富多彩的民族文化，而且有助于增进与南亚东南亚国家的理解与交流，为"一带一路"倡议的实施做出贡献。

云南师范大学外国语学院很重视这一领域的工作。在外国语学院领导支持下，李昌银教授带领一个由教授和中青年学者组成的团队对精选出来的17部云南少数民族经典作品进行英译，计划在5年内（"十三五"期间）翻译出版。这是一项十分有意义的宏大工程。

这17部民族典籍，内容全部为各民族的英雄史诗或神话传说，具有很高的历史意义和文学价值。这些作品涉及阿昌族、白族、傣族、德昂族、哈尼族、景颇族、拉祜族、苗族、纳西族、普米族、彝族等 11 个少数民族。

云南师范大学这支翻译队伍实力强大，主要由一些多年从事翻译教学、研究和实践的教授和副教授组成，他们是李昌银、黄瑛、彭庆华、孙兴文、吴相如、刘德周、杨慧芳、郜菊、陈萍、包琼（Joan Boulerice）等国内外专家学者。他们在云南翻译界都是风云人物。

在民族典籍英译中，这支队伍异军突起，为我国民族典籍英译壮大了声势，必将为中国民族典籍走向世界而成为世界文学的一部分做出新贡献。

民族典籍翻译与研究事业关乎国家的稳定统一，关乎民族关系的和谐发展，关乎世界多元文化的实现。在中国，民族典籍资源极为丰富，有待进一步挖掘、翻译。因此，民族典籍英译前景光明。同时，我们也应意识到，仍有许多濒临消失的少数民族典籍亟待拯救，民族典籍翻译与研究工作任重而道远。

（李正栓，中国英汉语比较研究会典籍英译专业委员会常务副会长兼秘书长）

Foreword by Li Zhengshuan

The translation of Chinese ethnic classics is an important approach in spreading Chinese culture, literature and civilization. It is a crucial component of Chinese culture going global. The spreading of Chinese culture and literature is a national policy and an important way to improve the cultural soft power of China. It plays an indispensable role in the cultural exchange between China and other countries and the development of world literature.

The ethnic groups in China have countless excellent classics with high anthropological, literary and cultural value. The ancestors of each ethnic group have passed down their distinctive culture orally or in writing. Almost all the ethnic groups have their own story of creation, epics, myths and legends.

Chinese ethnic classics are unique and irreplaceable. It is imperative to attach importance to the translation and research of ethnic classics; to explore the excellent ethnic cultures; to protect the civilization of ethnic groups; to enhance the communication and understanding among ethnic groups; to further spread the outstanding culture of ethnic groups to other parts of the world; and to build the cultural strength of China. Many ethnic groups live in the border areas and thus play an important role in the cultural and economic cooperation between China and its neighbors in the context of the Belt and Road Initiative.

Chinese ethnic classics are an important component of the magnificence and diversity of world culture. It is diversity that makes the world so colorful. The cultural diversity of Chinese ethnic classics has greatly enriched the world's pluralism and its distinctive features. People around the world have formed a new understanding of diversity. This diversity has expanded people's horizon and enriched their way of thinking. Digging out the educational and cultural value in these classics can contribute to the construction of China's self-confidence in culture.

The special value of the ethnic classics itself is of great significance to the strengthening of national culture and intercultural communication between China and foreign countries. The translation of ethnic classics is not just a literary exchange, but also a form of cultural communication. It is diplomacy through literature in that it consolidates the cultural ties between China and other countries.

After the founding of the People's Republic of China, the central government attached great importance to the translation and research of ethnic classics, provided the a great deal of policy support, and adopted a series of effective measures to speed up the process of rescuing, collating, translating and studying ethnic classics. The central government has convened several working conferences on Tibet and Xinjiang. In recent years, both China and other countries have paid close attention to multiculture. The translation of ethnic classics has become a hot topic.

In recent years, the translation and research of ethnic classics have progressed rapidly and have shown good prospects. The government strongly supports and grants the research projects of the national social science fund. The Ministry of Education and the State Ethnic Affairs Commission are also issuing research projects and giving funding to a large number of researchers. Many research projects on ethnic classics have been approved and carried out. Many ethnic classics have been translated into Chinese, English and other languages and published. More and more professionals have dedicated themselves to this new sphere of learning.

In this context, the academic conferences on translation of ethnic classics are held one after another all around the country. And up to now three have been held.

Yunnan is the province which has the most ethnic groups in China. Besides Han people, there are 25 ethnic groups, each with a population of more than 5,000. Among them, 15 ethnic groups are unique to Yunnan, which are the Bai, the Hani, the Dai, the Lisu, the Wa, the Lahu, the Naxi, the Jingpo, the Bulang, the Pumi, the Achang, the Jinuo, the Nu, the De'ang and the Dulong. Among these, 84% of the total number of the Bai people in China and 95% of the other 14 ethnic groups are living in Yunnan.

Yunnan is also the province which has the most cross-border ethnic groups. Of the 25 ethnic groups, 16 live across the border, namely: the Dai, the Zhuang, the Miao, the Jingpo, the Yao, the Hani, the De'ang, the Wa, the Lahu, the Yi, the Achang, the Lisu, the Buyi, the Nu, the Bulang and the Dulong.

The ethnic groups in Yunnan have created splendid cultures. According to statistics, the number of classics of Yunnan ethnic groups is more than 100 thousand volumes and classics in oral tradition are more than 40 thousand. In order to save and protect these ancient books, the Office of Classics Collation and Publishing of Yunnan Ethnic Groups Affairs Commission planned to compile and publish 100 volumes of *A Collection of Yunnan Ethnic Group Rare Books* in five years, which is an ambitious plan. The introduction of the ancient classics via translation can not only promote and develop the colorful ethnic cultures of Yunnan, but also contribute to the understanding and exchange between China and countries in South Asia and Southeast Asia and to the implementation of the Belt and Road Initiative as well.

The School of Foreign Languages and Literature of Yunnan Normal University is paying close attention to this field. With the support of the School and the University, Professor Li Changyin is leading a group of professors and young scholars to do the project of *"Classics of Yunnan Ethnic Groups in English Translation"*, which includes 17 ethnic classics selected carefully from Yunnan's bountiful ethnic classics. These books are the heroic epics or myths and legends of each ethnic groups with great historical significance and literary value. They will finish the translation in five years (during "the thirteenth five-year plan"). After that, all the works will be published by Yunnan People's Publishing House.

The 17 works cover 11 ethnic groups: the Achang, the Bai, the Dai, the De'ang, the Hani, the Jingpo, the Lahu, the Miao, the Naxi, the Pumi and the Yi. All of these groups except the Miao and the Yi are unique to Yunnan.

The translation team of Yunnan Normal University is full of strength and vitality, composed of professors and associate professors who have been occupied in translation teaching, research, and practice for a long time. They are Li Changyin, Huang Ying, Peng Qinghua, Sun Xingwen, Wu Xiangru, Liu Dezhou, Yang Huifang, Gao Ju, Chen Ping, Joan Boulerice and other experts and scholars who are representative figures in the translation field in Yunnan province.

This team is a new force that has suddenly arisen in terms of translating ethnic classics. It is expanding the momentum of ethnic classics translation in China and has made a new contribution for China's ethnic classics to go global and become a part of world literature.

The translation and research of ethnic classics are related to the development of Chinese culture and the realization of multiculturalism in the world. In China, ethnic classics are extremely rich in resources, which require us to make further exploration and research and translate them into other languages. Therefore, the future of translating ethnic classics is bright. At the same time, we should also realize that there are still many ethnic works which are close to extinction and urgently need to be rescued. We still have a long way to go in the fields of translation and research in ethnic classics.

(Li Zhengshuan, Standing Vice Chairman and Secretary General, Classics Translation Committee of CACSEC)

序 二

◎王 宏

好友云南师范大学外国语学院李昌银教授来电嘱托我为"云南少数民族经典作品英译文库"的出版写一序言，并随即发来该文库的背景资料，让我"不着急，慢慢写"。我本人从事中国典籍英译及研究，深知少数民族典籍对外传译的重要性，但又是少数民族典籍翻译的门外汉。因此，我是怀着虚心学习的态度来写此序言的。近年来，在中国文化"走出去"战略工程大背景下，在中央和地方各级政府的大力支持下，我国少数民族典籍的对外传译及研究工作顺利开展，取得了很大的进步。请看以下数据：

2008年，广西百色学院韩家权教授获批国家社科基金项目《布洛陀史诗》（壮汉英对照）。该项目已顺利结项，并于2013年12月获得中国民间文艺最高奖"山花奖"。

2012年，广西百色学院外语系翻译团队翻译的国家级非物质文化遗产《壮族嘹歌》（英文版）由广西师范大学出版社正式出版。

2012年，东北大学秦皇岛分校吴松林教授主编的《蒙古族系列：江格尔（汉英对照）》（上下册）由吉林大学出版社出版。

2013年，河北师范大学李正栓教授英译《藏族格言诗》

由长春出版社出版发行。

2013年，云南财经大学崔晓霞教授撰写的《〈阿诗玛〉英译研究》收入由王宏印教授主编、民族出版社出版的"民族典籍翻译研究丛书"。

2014年，东北大学秦皇岛分校吴松林教授撰写的《满族档案文献研究》申请到国家社科后期资助，他英译的《英雄格斯尔可汗》由吉林大学出版社出版。

2014年，中南民族大学张立玉教授主持的"土家族主要典籍英译及研究"获批国家社科基金项目。

2015年，西安外国语大学梁真惠副教授撰写的《〈玛纳斯〉翻译传播研究》收入由王宏印教授主编、民族出版社出版的"民族典籍翻译研究丛书"。

与此同时，第一届和第二届全国少数民族典籍英译学术研讨会分别于2012年和2014年在广西民族大学和大连民族学院举行，参加会议的院校分布之广、与会代表数量之众、提交论文数量之多和涉及研究话题之细，十分可喜。2016年还将在中南民族大学举行第三届全国少数民族典籍英译学术研讨会。

为什么少数民族典籍的对外传译及研究工作在短短几年就受到译界的青睐，取得众多成果？我认为，这在很大程度上归于典籍翻译界乃至翻译界同仁对"中国典籍"的重新思考和认识。中国典籍浩如烟海，卷帙浩繁，举世瞩目，是全人类共同的精神财富。但对于中国典籍的理解，我们以前较多限于汉民族的重要文献和书籍，而对少数民族多有忽略。在讨论中国典籍时，也较多关注古代文学作品。其实，中国典籍指"中国清代末年1911年以前的重要文献和书籍",这就要求我们从事典籍翻译时,不但要翻译古代文学典籍作品,还要翻译古代哲学、科技、法律、医学、经济、军事、天文、地理等诸多方面的典籍作品,不但要翻译汉民族的典籍作品,也要翻译各少数民族的典籍作品。

民族典籍具有该民族的原型符号的特质,蕴藏着能够"遗传"并不断"再生"的文化基因。民族典籍是中华传统文化的内核,同时还是中华传统文化的符号构成规则。中国是具有56个民族的多民族国家,少数民族典籍是我国少数民族勤劳与智慧的结晶,是中华文明、也是世界文明不可或缺的一部分。少数民族典籍对外传译具有跨文化交流的作用,它不但有助于更多的人了解少数民族的独特文化,而且还有助于保护少数民族文化的独特性、维持少数民族文化多样性、促进各民族团结、提升中华文化软实力等。

中国少数民族典籍涉及宗教、文学、历史、语言、医学、天文历算等领域,内容丰富,版本多样,载体特殊,传承奇特。仅以《中国少数民族古籍总目提要》为例,该书于1997年正式立项,全书总体设计约60卷、110册,目前已出版23个民族卷共20册:纳西族卷、白族卷、东乡族卷·裕固族卷·保安族卷、土族卷·撒拉族卷、锡伯族卷、哈尼族卷、回族卷·铭刻、柯尔克孜族卷、羌族卷、毛南族卷·京族卷、仫佬族卷、达斡尔族卷、土家族卷、鄂温克族卷、鄂伦春族卷、赫哲族卷、苗族卷、侗族卷、黎族卷、朝鲜族卷。该书真实地反映了我国各少数民族古籍赋存的全面情况,充实了中国的历史和文化内容,为后人探索各种文化形式的源流、揭示中国社会文化发展的轨迹提供了极为珍贵的资料，为我国乃至世界各国人文科学研究提供了一套新颖而全面的资料，对于弘扬中华民族传统文化具有深远的历史意义和现实意义。

少数民族典籍的对外传译是一项艰巨的工作，涉及将少数民族语言译成汉语、少数民族语言之间的互译和少数民族语言译成外语（主要是英语）。前两类翻译历史源远流长，最早可追溯到春秋战国时代《越人歌》的翻译，即汉、壮语之间的翻译。少数民族典籍译成外语的时间则要晚一些。据考证，维吾尔族古典长诗《福乐智慧》成书于1069年或1070年，目前尚未发现完整的原稿，只存留下来三个抄本，分别为赫拉特抄本、费尔干纳抄本与埃及抄本，其中费尔干纳抄本于12~13世纪用阿拉伯文纳斯赫体抄写，1914年发现于今中亚乌孜别克斯坦纳曼干城，现存于该共和国科学院东方研究所。这是少数民族典籍译介到国外的最早纪录。少数民族典籍外译在现代有了较快发展。一些少数民族典籍，如藏族的《格萨尔王传》、蒙古族的《江格尔》和柯尔克孜族的《玛纳斯》等英雄史诗，云南彝族的《阿诗玛》、维吾尔族的《艾里甫和赛乃姆》等民间叙事长诗已先后被翻译成英语及其他外国文字，为世人所知。这对传承少数民族经典，推动中外文化交流起到了不可替代的作用。然而，还有大量的中国少数民族典籍等待我们去翻译和研究。

云南省少数民族典籍资源十分丰富。据不完全统计，云南少数民族文字文献古籍蕴藏量达10万余册（卷），口传古籍4万余种。"云南少数民族经典作品英译文库"正是依托云南省丰富的少数民族典籍资源，借助云南师范大学外国语学院强大的翻译师资队伍，在云南人民出版社的有力支持下，首次将云南少数民族经典作品成系列对外译介的大力举措。云南师范大学外国语学院对"云南少数民族经典作品英译文库"十分重视，他们首先邀请省内外少数民族语言文化研究专家对云南民族典籍和民族文化经典作品进行筛选，做到"好中选好，优中选优"，同时调配最强的翻译力量承担文库的翻译任务。我粗略看了该文库的选题，发现选题面广，覆盖范围宽，收入了云南省阿昌族、白族、傣族、纳西族、德昂族、哈尼族、景颇族、拉祜族、苗族、普米族和彝族等民族的典籍作品。云南共有25个少数民族，其中11个少数民族的典籍作品都覆盖到了，不少作品还是首次译成英文。这将彻底改变云南少数民族典籍由于对外译介数量较少，不为世界了解的尴尬局面。

对于云南师范大学外国语学院而言，把少数民族典籍英译作为翻译专业的优势特色进行建设，这将对该院的学科建设起到助推作用。"云南少数民族经典作品英译文库"所产生的翻译成果和研究成果将培养出一批优秀的典籍翻译和研究团队，凸显该院在全国的学术特色和学术影响，同时还能将翻译能力和研究能力转化为教学能力，提高云南师范大学外国语学院翻译专业研究生的培养质量，为社会输送高水平的翻译人才，有力地支撑学院翻译专业学科的建设和发展。我对云南师范大学外国语学院的翻译师资队伍较为熟悉。作为云南省唯一获得省级高校优势特色学科建设项目的外国语学院，该院具有雄厚的翻译师资力量，在云南省各高校中当属第一。多年来，该院翻译与跨文化研究团队一直承担着对外交流与合作的各种口笔译项目及任务。由外国语学院精心挑选和确定的"云南少数民族经典作品英译文库"翻译人员绝大多数都是云南省翻译领域里的知名教授或专家，有国外留学经历，且具有扎实的英汉双语语言功底，曾翻译出版多部译著和翻译作品，并且主持和参与过多项翻译项目的研究。我阅读李昌银教授发来的文库翻译人员名单，发现多名我所熟悉的知名教授、博士也在其中，感到格外放心。

"云南少数民族经典作品英译文库"的出版发行是云南省翻译界的一件大事，也是我国少数民族典籍翻译传来的又一佳音。想当年，我和《大中华文库》总协调人李林老师曾在参加全国典籍英译学术研讨会之余一起找到李昌银教授，敦促李教授向学校和同事呼吁，少数民族典籍翻译及研究是富矿，值得快挖、深挖，能早出成果，出大成果。今天，我们当年的心愿变成了美好的现实，心里感到特别高兴。再次热烈祝贺"云南少数民族经典作品英译文库"的顺利出版！

（王宏，中国典籍翻译研究会副会长、苏州大学博士生导师）

Foreword by Wang Hong

My friend Professor Li Changyin of Yunnan Normal University asked me to write a few words for the publication of *Classics of Yunnan Ethnic Groups in English Translation*. I am more than delighted to do it. As I have been doing research in the English translation of Chinese classics, I know how important his work is. In recent years, substantial progress has been made in translating Chinese ethnic classics into English and other foreign languages. Books published in this respect include *The Liao Songs of the Zhuang Nationality* (Nanning: Guangxi Normal University Press, 2008, English Edition), *Mongolian Series: Jianggeer* (Changchun: Jilin University Press, 2012, Bilingual Edition), *Tibetan Gnomic Verses Translated into English* (Changchun: Changchun Press, 2013), and *Geser Khan: a Hero* (Changchun: Jilin University Press, 2014). Several projects in the English translation of ethnic classics have received funding from the National Planning Office of Philosophy and Social Science and, as a result, a number of monographs and PhD dissertations have been published.

Meanwhile, it is encouraging to see that the first conferences on English translation of ethnic classics in China have been held in Guangxi Nationalities University and

Dalian Nationalities Institute respectively. Participants were both many and enthusiastic. Many papers were presented and a lot of topics discussed. The third conference will be hosted by South Central Nationalities University in 2016.

Why, then, has this field attracted so much attention from translators and scholars alike and accomplished so much in just a few years? The answer, I believe, lies in a rethinking of what constitutes Chinese classics as an indispensable part of human heritage. We used to see Chinese classics as more or less equal to the classics of the Han people, excluding works by other ethnic groups. Moreover, when we talk about Chinese classics, we focus too much on the literary works of ancient times. Yet Chinese classics actually refer to "important works and books before 1911, the year when the Qing dynasty fell, bringing an end to imperial rule." This definition requires us to pay attention not just to literary works, but also writings in other subjects, such as philosophy, science, law, medicine, economics, military affairs, astronomy, and geography, not only Han works, but writings by other ethnic groups as well.

The classical works of a nation are its archetypal symbols, the major carriers of its cultural genes. Chinese classics make up the core of Chinese tradition. The Chinese nation consists of 56 ethnic groups. Ethnic classics are an important part of not only Chinese traditional culture, but also of world civilization. The translation of these works into other languages is important in that it helps to promote cross-cultural communications between China and other countries and to protect and preserve the uniqueness and diversity of ethnic cultures by making them accessible to foreign readers.

Chinese ethnic classics cover a variety of areas, such as religion, literature, history, language, medicine, astrology, and calendar, with numerous editions, special media and unique ways of transmission from generation to generation. Take, for example, *An Anthology of Chinese Ethnic Classics*, a colossal project that includes 110 volumes, 20 of which, from 23 ethnic groups, have been published. The anthology reflects the variety and quantity of China's ethnic classics and provides valuable material and resources for studying, understanding and developing Chinese culture and history in a more comprehensive and sustainable way.

The translation of Chinese ethnic classics into foreign languages is a very demanding job, involving rendering from ethnic languages to Chinese, between ethnic languages, and from ethnic languages (often via Chinese) to foreign languages. The first two types of translation can be traced back to the Spring and Autumn Period, when *The Song of the Yue People* was translated from their mother tongue into Chinese. The earliest translation of ethnic classics into a foreign language is *Wisdom of Royal Glory*, a long poem of the Uygurs, which was rendered from the source language into Arabic and is now in the Oriental Institute of Uzbekistan at Namangan. But it was not until modern times that the translation of ethnic classics into foreign languages accelerated. Noticeably, ethnic epics, such as *The Story of Prince Geser* of the Tibetans, *The Story of Jianggeer* of the Mongolians, *Manas* of the Kyrgyz, and narrative poems such as *Ashima* of the Yi people, *Alip and Salam* of the Uygurs, etc., have been published. These translations have contributed to acquainting the world with Chinese ethnic classics, but many remain to be translated.

Yunnan is rich in ethnic classics, boasting more than 100 thousand volumes of written classics and over 40 thousand pieces of oral literature. Relying on such bountiful resources, as a collective endeavor of the translation team of the School of Foreign Languages and Literature, Yunnan Normal University and with the help of Yunnan People's Publishing House, *Classics of Yunnan Ethnic Groups in English Translation* is the first project to translate Yunnan ethnic classics into English on a large scale. The School adheres to a professional spirit and academic standard in carrying out the project by selecting the most authoritative texts in the source language (Chinese) and recruiting the best translators from its huge faculty. The selection of the works, covering eleven of the twenty-five ethnic groups of the province, indicates expertise and insight. The implementation of the project will change the embarrassing obscurity of Yunnan ethnic classics by making them known to the world, many of them for the first time.

In light of disciplinary development, the project is of

great importance, too. Participating in the translation will strengthen the academic foundation of the teachers, enrich their experience and enhance their translation skills and research ability. This in turn will help them become better teachers and thus able to educate students with higher quality. The publication of the books will add greatly to the faculty accomplishments of the School and raise the academic standing of Yunnan Normal University by taking the first step in this direction among the universities of Yunnan province.

This publication project is a great event not only for Yunnan itself, but also for China. Looking back, I remember that Professor Li Changyin, our friend Li Lin, editor of the *Library of Chinese Classics*, and I talked enthusiastically about initiating something like this in Yunnan when we attended a conference on the translation of ethnic classics in Soochow. Lin and I strongly suggested that Professor Li do it as soon as possible. Now I am very pleased to see our talk becoming reality. Again, my congratulations on the publication of *Classics of Yunnan Ethnic Groups in English Translation*!

(Wang Hong, PhD supervisor at Soochow University, Vice Chairman of Classics Translation Committee of CACSEC)

支萨·甲布 // Zhisa Jiabu

General Introduction

This publication project, Classics of *Yunnan Ethnic Groups in English Translation*, aims at introducing Yunnan ethnic classical works to the world by making them available to native speakers of English who might be interested in them. With the publication of the *Library of Chinese Classics*, which consists only of books written by Han authors in classical Chinese, attention now is being turned to the English translation and publication of ethnic classics, books produced by ethnic writers about their history and culture. Universities in provinces such as Guangxi, Guizhou, Liaoning, Xinjiang, and Xizang, have taken the initiative. We in Yunnan must do something, because Yunnan has the largest number of ethnic groups in China. 15 of the 25 ethnic groups in the province, the Bai, the Dai, the Hani, the Lisu, the Wa, the Lahu, the Naxi, the Jingpo, the Bulang, the Pumi, the Achang, the Jinuo, the Nu, the De'ang, and the Dulong, live in no other place but Yunnan. The classics of these people, either in their own languages or in Chinese translations, are a great treasure house, which should be accessible to English readers and scholars. But what works should be translated first?

All the 25 ethnic groups in Yunnan have their classics, epics, mythology, creation stories, folksongs, folk drama, mountain songs, and funeral lament lyrics, most of which exist in different versions in different places. According to one estimation, there are more than 100 thousand volumes of them, excluding those in oral form. After a thorough survey and extensive consultations with experts of ethnic studies, we concluded that priority must be given to epics and mythologies, as they reflect an ethnic people's philosophy, history and culture more than anything else by narrating the stories of where and how they think they came from. From many epics and mythologies, we selected 17 of the most authoritative and popular classics representing 11 Yunnan ethnic groups, the Yi, the Bai, the Miao, the Hani, the Lahu, the Naxi, the Jingpo, the Pumi, the Achang, the Dai, and the De'ang. These works are all in Chinese, translated from the original by bilingual scholars whose mother tongue is their own ethnic language and who are fluent and proficient in Chinese. Some were recorded from their oral form at rituals and performances. We did not choose texts written in the ethnic language, not least because it is very hard to find a translator who is skilled in both the ethnic language and English. Moreover, some of the classics in the ethnic language were circulated in various oral forms and fragments. The published Chinese versions have been carefully edited and translated, hence they are more reliable. The next question is: how to translate them?

It happens that all of the 17 works except one are in

支萨·甲布 // Zhisa Jiabu

verse form, with lines more or less the same length and loose rhymes, but no regular meter. A poem must be rendered into a poem; anything less is unacceptable. So here are the general rules we follow when doing the translation.

One. If the original is verse, the translated text must be verse, too.

Two. Reproduce the ideas and the images of the original as completely as possible.

Three. Reproduce the figures of speech of the original as much as possible.

Four. Do not change the number of lines in a stanza unless absolutely necessary.

Five. Do not use standard meters in English, because the Chinese original does not follow any regular meter. Use the natural rhythm of English instead, but most of the lines should look more or less the same length.

Six. Do not use rhyme unless it comes naturally and is faithful to the content of the original.

What we try to do is, to use Susan Bassnett's words, "transplant the seed", not the tree itself. As for the various aspects of form, particularly meter and end rhyme, we reproduce them when it is possible and abandon them when it is necessary.

Who will do the translations? As this is a collective project of the School of Foreign Languages and Literature of Yunnan Normal University, our team consists of a dozen faculty members and two students from our MA translation program who are already teachers in other universities. All the translators have been teaching translation and doing translation research for a long time. They have published not just academic articles on translation, but also translated books from English to Chinese or vice versa.

Traditionally, people translate into their mother tongue, not into a foreign language. But the situation is changing. Many translators today are translating from their mother tongue into a foreign language. The quality can be good, as Nike K. Pokorn and Stuart Campbell prove in *Challenging the Traditional Axioms: Translation into a non-mother tongue* (Amsterdam: John Benjamins Publishing Company, 2005) and *Translation into the Second Language* (New York: Routledge, 2013) respectively. The case of China provides further evidence for their argument. The translation of Chinese classics into English was initiated by James Legge and Herbert Allen Giles in the 19th century and carried on in the 20th century by Arthur Waley, David Hawkes, Burton Watson, John Minford, Stephen Owen and others. It is noticeable that these English and American sinologists were soon joined by Chinese scholars residing in the West, such as Hongming (Tomson) Gu and Lin Yutang, among others. They took up the job because they thought it was their obligation to give English readers more faithful translations than Western sinologists could, who, as their target language is their mother tongue, often misinterpret the original text and misrepresent Chinese culture. Since the 1950s, there has been an increasingly powerful trend for Mainland Chinese translators to render or re-render Chinese classics into foreign languages, English in particular. In our time, this work is gathering momentum, enthusiastically advocated and actively practiced by such well-known translation experts as Yang Xianyi of Beijing Foreign Language Press, Xu Yuanchong of Beijing University, Wang Rongpei of Dalian Foreign Language Institute, Wang Hongyin of Nankai University, Wang Hong of Soochow University, Li Zhengshuan of Hebei Normal University, and many more. These professors are not just translators, but also scholars in translation studies. More importantly, some of them, Xu Yuanchong, Wang Hong and Li Zhengshuan, for example, have had their translations published by Western publishers, which suggests that their English meets the international standard.

In the case of our project, we request that the translators do their best to produce good translations. When they submit them to us, they should represent the highest level that they can attain. Then the general editors appointed by the School read the translated texts and remove inaccurate renderings and grammar mistakes if there are any. On top of that, we've taken an indispensable measure to ensure that our English is readable. We asked Ms. Joan Cecile Boulerice, an American teacher who has been teaching English in our school since

2009, to read every text that we've translated and improve the English by making it more natural and idiomatic. This is the best we can do. Of course any problems that still remain in the translations are ours. They have nothing to do with our American teacher.

As the project is well under way, we would like to thank all those who have helped to make it possible. Ms Guo Muyu, director of the South and Southeast Asia Editorial Department, Yunnan People's Publishing House, has been most helpful in our cooperation. In addition, she has added importance to the project by turning it into a national publication project. Yunnan Normal University has supported us by paying the publication fees so that the translators won't have to be burdened with the financial responsibilities for this project. Professor Li Zhengshuan and Professor Wang Hong not only have always encouraged us to go on but have also written the forewords for the project, putting it in a global perspective. Ms Joan Boulerice's revision has ensured the fluency of the translated texts. Finally, special thanks must be given to Professor Wang Hong, again, and Mr Li Lin of Hunan People's Press for their suggestion that has helped us conceive the project from the very beginning.

(The General Editors, School of Foreign Languages & Literature, Yunnan Normal University, Kunming)

支萨·甲布 // Zhisa Jiabu

A Brief Introduction to *Zhisa Jiabu*

Zhisa Jiabu is an important epic sung among the Pumi people. The epic tells the story of Zhisa Jiabu, an orphan. It describes how he was brought up by his aunt, how he got to know the stories and whereabouts of his parents, how he prepared for revenge, how he killed the monster who harassed his community and achieved revenge for his father and how he killed the demon who kidnapped his mother and saved his mother.

    The epic is divided into prologue, main body and epilogue. The prologue serves as an introduction to the epic, which says that the Pumi people should not forget their hero Zhisa Jiabu. The main body of the epic consists of six cantos. Canto 1 is about how Zhisa Jiabu was brought up by his aunt. Canto 2 describes Zhisa Jiabu's wish to know the whereabouts of his parents and how he used a clever plan to make his aunt tell the stories of his parents. Canto 3 tells the story of how a unicorn brought calamities to Zhisa Jiabu's neighborhoods and how Zhisa Jiabu's father died when he tried to kill the monster. Canto 4 tells the story of the demon kidnapping Zhisa Jiabu's mother. Canto 5 is about how Zhisa Jiabu trained hard and then killed the monster after a tough fight and he got revenge for his father. Canto 6 describes how Zhisa Jiabu found his mother and killed the demon with help from his mother. In the epilogue, it is pointed out that the Pumi people will never forget their own hero Zhisa Jiabu.

The Translator

支萨·甲布

目录

序　歌 // 2

第一章 // 4

第二章 // 8

第三章 // 18

第四章 // 26

第五章 // 30

第六章 // 42

尾　歌 // 72

Zhisa Jiabu / Contents

Prologue // 3

Canto 1 // 5

Canto 2 // 9

Canto 3 // 19

Canto 4 // 27

Canto 5 // 31

Canto 6 // 43

Epilogue // 73

支萨·甲布 Zhisa Jiabu

是普米族人民广泛传唱的一部重要英雄史诗。

Zhisa Jiabu is an important epic sung among the Pumi people.

序　歌

今晚火塘为什么又暖又亮？
因为我把心中的柴火添上。
记忆像石磨从遥远的年代转起，
我要把普米英雄的故事传唱。

是大山的儿子，
要知道大山的脾气；
是普米人的后代，
就要知道祖先英雄的事迹。

支萨·甲布是普米的儿子，
支萨·甲布是普米的英雄，
他像一颗发光的宝石，
永远闪亮在普米人的心里。

Prologue

Why is the fireplace so warm and bright?
I have added firewood in my heart for more light.
Like a stone mill my story starts from ancient times;
I'll sing a story about Pumi heroes tonight.

The sons of mountains
Must know the temper of mountains;
Pumi offspring
Must know their ancestors' heroic deeds.

Zhisa Jiabu was a son of the Pumi;
Zhisa Jiabu was a hero of the Pumi.
Like a bright gem,
He shines forever in the hearts of the Pumi.

第一章

普米人的支萨·甲布,
从小失去了亲生父母。
好心的孃孃抚养他,
把多磨的时光苦度。

清晨披着金灿灿的阳光,
到山间草地去放羊;
夜晚围着暖暖的火塘,
听孃孃把普米古礼① 讲唱。

荞麦熟了三回,
杜鹃花开了三度。
甲布长得像云间的大雁,
甲布长得像雪山的金鹿。
既有阿妈的美丽和善良,
又有阿爸的心胆和筋骨。

---

① 古礼:指古老的传说故事、礼仪习俗的来历等。

Canto 1

Pumi's Zhisa Jiabu
Lost his parents in his childhood.
His kindhearted aunt brought him up,
Going through a tortuous time.

Along with golden sunlight at dawn,
He went to herd sheep on alpine meadows;
Sitting beside the warm fireplace when the sun was gone,
His aunt had ancient Pumi stories and customs sung.

Buckwheat was harvested three times;
Azalea flowers bloomed three times.
Jiabu looked like a wild goose in the clouds;
Jiabu looked like a golden deer in the snow mountains.
He had his mother's beauty and kindness
And his father's bravery and physique in his prime.

甲布出没在深山，
性情像阿爸那样果敢；
甲布操练在草坝，
武艺像阿爸那样精湛。

他发现天地是那么宽广，
山林是那样迷人。
他要到天地间磨炼，
他要到山林间追捕群狼。

Jiabu adventured in the mountains

As courageously and resolutely as his dad;

Jiabu practiced on the plains,

His martial arts as superb as his dad's.

He found so broad was the world,

And so fascinating were the mountain forests.

He wanted to steel himself in the world,

To pursue and capture wolves in the mountain forests.

第二章

地上的草木，
怎能没有种子？
世间的人群，
怎会没有父母？
甲布和孃孃为何这样孤独？
甲布要寻找自己的根骨。

孃孃见甲布还年幼，
父母的真情藏在心中。
每当甲布问起自己的父母，
孃孃总是咽下心酸的眼泪。

甲布不知父母的下落，
甲布不明爹妈的去向，
心里像钻进了虫蚁，
日日夜夜无不思量。

三年三月过去了，

Canto 2

For grass and woods on the earth,

Without seeds how could they grow?

For people in the world,

Without parents how could they come into being?

Why were Jiabu and his aunt so lonely?

Jiabu was determined to find his parents.

His aunt thought Jiabu was still too young,

So she kept the truth and held her tongue.

Whenever Jiabu asked about his parents,

His aunt always swallowed sad tears.

Jiabu did not know what his parents had done;

He did not know where his parents had gone.

He felt as if he had insects in his heart;

Day and night he could not take his thought away.

Three years and three months had passed;

三春三夏过去了。
孃孃不把真情讲,
甲布的日子实在难熬。

一天,甲布站在火塘边,
手拿搅棒炒玉米。
孃孃坐在房檐下,
麻线织布缝麻衣。

甲布手拿木搅棒,
心里却把主意想。
他用搅棒撬开木楞缝,
隔着板壁喊孃孃:
"孃孃,你接过玉米尝尝,
我炒的玉米香不香?"

孃孃的手伸过木楞缝,
一捧滚烫的玉米放在她手中。
甲布抽出搅棒捏住孃孃手,
趁机询问父母的迹踪:

"好心的孃孃啊,
小树长成大树,
树根扎在山中,

Three springs and three summers weren't spent fast.
His aunt did not tell him the truth;
Jiabu's life was not easy indeed.

One day, beside the fireplace Jiabu stood,
With a stick in his hand to stir their food of fried corn.
His aunt was sitting below the eaves,
Weaving linen threads to sew sleeves.

In his hand Jiabu had the stirring stick;
In his mind he came up with a trick.
Between logs, with the stick, a gap was pried;
He called his aunt behind the logs:
"Auntie, please taste these corn I fried,
To see if they are as delicious as those you fried?"

When his aunt's hand came through the hole,
A handful of hot corn was put into her palm.
Jiabu pulled the stick away and his aunt's hand was stuck;
Jiabu once again inquired the whereabouts of his parents:

"My kindhearted auntie,
When a small tree grows into a big one,
It is still deeply rooted in the mountain,

大树忘不了大山的恩情。

"善良的孃孃啊,
禾苗长出了谷粒,
禾根扎在地里,
谷米忘不了大地的哺育。"

"甲布已长大成人,
是父母把我生养。
我要寻找自己的生父,
我要孝敬自己的亲娘。"

孃孃的手被木缝卡紧,
孃孃的手被炒玉米烫疼。
她受不了剧烈的疼痛,
讲出甲布父母的实情。

"甲布啊,坚强的甲布,
小树长成了大树,
要为青山添色增彩;
孩儿长成了大人,
要把父母的恩仇记住。

"你的父亲叫支萨,

And it will never forget the kindness of the mountain.

"My kind auntie,

When seedlings grow and begin to produce grains,

Their roots are still in the ground,

And grains will never forget the nurture of the ground.

"Jiabu is already grown up;

My life is given by my parents.

I have to find my father;

I have to show my filial piety to my mother."

His aunt's hand was stuck between the logs,

And it hurt because of the hot corn kernels.

It was too painful to bear;

She began to tell the truth.

"Dear Jiabu, strong Jiabu,

When saplings grow into big trees,

They should add greenery and color to the mountains;

When a child grows into a grown-up,

He has to remember his parents' hatred."

"Your father was called Zhisa;

生性勇敢又坚强。
你的母亲叫娜姆,
心地聪明又善良。

"支萨是个好猎手,
精湛的武艺世无双。
娜姆美丽又勤劳,
心灵比容貌更漂亮。

"银白的月亮,
星星来做伴。
苍翠的大山,
白云相绕缠。

"蜜蜂把鲜花亲吻,
鱼儿把江河依恋。
支萨爱娜姆的美丽善良,
娜姆爱支萨的忠诚勇敢。

"支萨进山狩猎谋生路,
带回猎物一同尝;
娜姆日夜操劳做家务,
和睦更觉饭菜香。

He was brave and strong.
Your mother was Namu;
She is clever and kind."

"Zhisa was a good hunter,
Whose martial arts were matchless.
Namu was beautiful and diligent,
Her soul even more beautiful than her appearance."

"The silver-white moon
Has stars as its companions.
Green mountains
Are entwined by white clouds."

"Bees kiss flowers,
And fish love rivers.
Zhisa loved Namu's beauty and kindness;
Namu loved Zhisa's loyalty and bravery."

"In the mountains Zhisa went hunting,
Bringing prey to share with his darling.
Day and night Namu took care of housekeeping;
Their harmony made food more appetizing."

"狂风吹不散他俩的恩爱,
冰雪冻不坏他俩的衷情。
爱情像永不熄灭的火塘,
温暖着两颗真诚的心。

"过了三年又三月,
过了三冬又三夏。
在一个晴朗的早晨,
娜姆生下一个胖娃娃。

"父亲给你取名叫甲布①,
是要你像父亲一样刚强;
母亲给你取名叫甲布,
是要你像母亲一样善良。

"你吮吸着母亲的乳汁,
你承受着青山的滋养,
给阿妈带来了欢笑,
给阿爸增添了力量。
金鸟和银鸟比翼飞翔,
金花和银花竞相开放。"

---

① 甲布:具有坚强、勇敢之意,是普米族老人给男孩子取名时的常用尊名。

"Gales could not blow away their conjugal love;
Ice was unable to freeze their heartfelt feelings.
Like inextinguishable fire,
Their love warmed two loyal hearts."

"Three years and three months were gone;
Three winters and three summers were done.
On a sunny morning,
Namu gave birth to a cute baby."

"Your father named you Jiabu[①],
Hoping you would be as brave as he.
Your mother called you Jiabu,
Hoping you would be as kind as she.

"Sucking your mother's milk,
And enjoying the nourishment of the mountains,
You brought laughter to your mother,
And added strength to your father.
Golden birds and silver birds flew side by side;
Golden flowers and silver flowers bloomed far and wide."

[①] Jiabu means being strong and brave; it is a name that old Pumi people often give to their children.

第三章

"天空布满乌云,
万物遭受厄运。
大地一片混乱,
灾难处处降临。

"天与地之间,
白龙王与黑龙王之间,
为争夺地权,
正在展开一场恶战。

"妖魔和鬼怪,
趁机显狰狞,
到处吃牲畜,
遍地吞咽人。

"在森林茂密的大山中,
一个大怪兽在作乱。
头上的独角力无穷,

Canto 3

"The sky was full of black clouds.
Everything suffered from disasters.
The earth was in chaos;
Disasters were everywhere."

"Between the earth and the sky,
Dragon Black and Dragon White,
For the control of land,
Started a fierce fight."

"Demons and monsters
Took advantage of the time.
They killed cattle,
And swallowed humans everywhere."

"In a dense forest in the mountains,
A huge monster brought endless disasters.
Its uni-horn horn had infinite power;

嘴里的利齿像刀尖。

"独角兽在山林中横行,
三乡四水的百姓快被吃尽。
没有一个人敢去拼杀,
没有一个人能把它战胜。

"支萨从小疾恶如仇,
支萨从小爱民如亲。
心里燃起冲天怒火,
决心除恶进山林。

"支萨精心饲养天马,
给天马备上银铃金鞍。
采来嫩草与山鸡肉相拌,
喂天马一日三餐。
不分昼夜在草坪上苦练,
天马一天能跑过九座高山。

"过去了三月三个夜晚,
过去了三月三个白天。
支萨带上强弩毒箭,
骑上天马进了深山。

Its teeth were as sharp as knife blades.

"With the monster seeking prey around the mountain forest,
Most people nearby were killed.
Nobody dared to challenge it;
Nobody could beat the beast."

"Zhisa hated evil like an enemy since childhood;
Zhisa loved people like family in the neighborhood.
He had a towering rage to the monster,
Determined to kill the monster in the woods.

"Zhisa fed his winged horse with great care,
And equipped it with silver bells and a golden saddle.
He cut tender grass and mixed it with pheasant meat
To feed the horse three times a day.
He practiced hard on the grassland night and day;
The horse could run the distance of nine mountains in a day."

"Three months and three nights were gone;
Three months and three days were done.
Bringing a powerful crossbow and poisoned arrows with him,
Zhisa rode the winged horse into the mountains."

"暗黑的天边乌云滚翻,
吃饱的怪物正呼呼入眠。
支萨拉开强弓硬弩,
搭上锋利的毒箭,
瞄准怪物的胸膛,
呼啸的毒箭飞向前方。

"怪物被飞来的毒箭惊醒,
竖起利角吼声震天。
张开大口飞动巨蹄,
猛扑到支萨跟前。

"支萨射出所有毒箭,
怪物越战越凶残,
支萨抽出长刀猛砍,
怪物的气势有增无减。

"怪物的皮肤有九层,
毒箭无法射穿;
怪物的脚有九双,
长刀不能砍断。

"支萨气势弱,
支萨力使完,

"Dark clouds were rolling on the horizon;

The satiated monster was sleeping.

Zhisa pulled his powerful crossbow,

Mounted a poisoned arrow,

Aimed at the monster's chest,

And then let the whistling arrow go."

"The monster was awakened by the arrow;

It raised its sharp horn and roared like thunder.

Opening its huge mouth and raising its huge hoofs,

The monster flew at Zhisa."

"Zhisa shot all his arrows,

But the monster became even more ferocious.

Zhisa drew out his long knife and cut heavily,

While the monster's momentum became greater but not less."

"The monster had nine layers of skin,

And poisoned arrows could not penetrate them;

The monster had nine pairs of feet,

Too hard for Zhisa's knife to cut them off."

"Zhisa lost his momentum

And ran out of strength.

怪物力无穷,
越战越凶顽。
利角刺进支萨胸膛,
支萨的鲜血染红了天边。

"漆黑的天边现出红霞,
那是支萨的鲜血浸染;
山林里传出声声呼唤,
那是乡亲们把支萨思念。"

The monster's strength was endless,

And became even more powerful.

Its sharp horn pierced Zhisa's chest,

And Zhisa's blood reddened the horizon."

"Red clouds appeared on the black horizon;

They were colored by Zhisa's blood.

Calls were heard in the woods;

They were the folks' memory of Zhisa."

第四章

"鲜花开了又谢,
树叶青了又黄。
日子过了三年三月,
岁月熬了三夏三春。

"大地还是一片混乱,
人间还是不得安宁。
娜姆的泪水还没干,
新的灾祸又降临。

"娜姆美丽的容颜像红杜鹃,
娜姆动人的眼睛像星星,
娜姆可爱的名字像朵香花,
芳馨传遍九山十箐。

"魔王听说娜姆的美名,
吃不爽口,睡不安身。
在一个风狂雨暴的夜晚,

Canto 4

"Flowers bloomed and withered,

And leaves became green and then yellow.

Three years and three months' time had passed;

Three summers and three springs were not spent fast."

"The land was still a mess;

The world was still lacking peace.

Before Namu's tears dried,

One more disaster came by."

"Namu's beautiful appearance was like a red Azalea flower;

Namu's touching eyes were like stars.

Namu's name was like a flower,

Whose fragrance spread over nine mountains and ten valleys."

"The Demon heard of Namu's beauty,

Unable to eat well and sleep soundly.

During a stormy night,

魔王抢走了娜姆——你的母亲。

"从此你失去了母爱,
跟着孃孃东躲西奔。
娜姆在魔洞伺候魔王,
不知如今是死是生。

"你父亲的天马飞进白玉海,
大青树下埋着银铃金鞍。
树洞中藏着锋利的长刀,
树枝上挂着弩弓毒箭。

"跨过九条大箐,
翻过九座高山。
山洞里有魔王的宫殿,
你母亲就关在里边。"

The Demon kidnapped Namu, your mother."

"You lost maternal love ever since,
Living with me, your aunt, in hiding and roaming.
Namu was forced to serve the Demon in his cave,
And we don't know if she is dead or alive."

"Your father's winged horse dove into White Jade Lake;
The silver bells and the golden saddle were buried under a big
    green tree.
His long sharp knife was hidden in a hole of the tree;
His crossbow and the poisoned arrows were hung on the branches."

"After crossing nine valleys,
And climbing nine mountains,
You will find the Demon's palace in the cave,
And your mother is locked in the palace. "

第五章

甲布弄清了父母的下落,
他要进山杀死怪兽和恶魔。
他要从魔洞救出母亲,
让人间永远免受灾祸。

从大青树下挖出银铃金鞍,
从大青树上取下弩弓毒箭,
从树洞中拿出宝刀,
甲布准备与怪兽恶魔决战。

甲布来到秀丽的山脚,
山背面的白玉海洁净碧蓝,
水面上没有一丝波纹,
青山和白云都倒映水面。

甲布遥望着海心,

Canto 5

Knowing his parents' whereabouts,
Jiabu was determined to kill the monster and the Demon.
He wanted to save his mother from the Demon's cave,
And to save the world from disasters forever.

Digging out the silver bells and the golden saddle from
    under the tree,
Picking the crossbow and poisoned arrows from the
    branches of the tree,
Taking out the precious knife from the hole in the tree,
Jiaba prepared to fight against the monster and the Demon.

Jiabu came to the foot of the beautiful mountain,
And found the crystal blue White Jade Lake.
There wasn't a ripple on the surface,
And green mountains and white clouds were reflected on it.

Towards the center of the lake,

支萨·甲布 // Zhisa Jiabu

放开喉咙高喊三声,
"打宗里呀哦休休!"①
声音飘过海面传到海心。

甲布的喊声回荡在山间,
一条裂缝出现在海面。
天马从海底慢慢升起,
亲热地来到甲布面前。

甲布骑着天马到山里,
找到怪兽的脚印比一比:
怪兽一步跃九丈,
天马只跨八丈九。

天马赛不过怪兽,
甲布不能去报仇。
他把天马牵回家,
精养苦练不罢休。

三春三夏又过去,
三年三月又到头。
天马长得英俊又健壮,
一步能跨九丈九。

---

① 普米语,意即我的天马呀快到身边来。

Jiabu shouted three times,
"Da-zong-li-ya-e-xiu-xiu!"①
His voice reached the center of the lake.

Jiabu's voice echoed among mountains,
And a rift appeared on the surface of the lake.
The winged horse rose slowly from the lake,
And came affectionately to Jiabu.

Jiabu rode the winged horse to the mountain,
Finding some footprints of the monster for comparison.
The monster could leap thirty meters;
The winged horse could not leap so far.

The winged horse could not race against the monster;
Jiabu could not go and take revenge on the monster.
He led the winged horse back home
To raise it carefully and steel himself hard.

Three springs and three summers were gone;
Three years and three months were done.
The winged horse became beautiful and strong,
And could jump thirty-three meters with a leap.

---

① Pumi language, which means "My winged horse, come to me quickly."

弓弩、长刀和毒箭,
挎在甲布的双肩;
装满毒血的猪尿泡,
拴在甲布的身前。
辞别嬢嬢骑上天马,
甲布奔向黑暗的天边。

甲布在深山找到了怪兽,
仇人间展开了生死的决斗。
怪兽的利角对甲布顶过来,
天马扬蹄闪到怪兽身后。

甲布仇恨的宝刀,
把身边的树木斩断。
怪兽坚硬的独角,
把周围的巨石顶翻。

朝前三个回合,
朝后三次交锋。
甲布越战越猛,
怪兽越斗越凶。

从太阳东升,

With his crossbow, long knife and poisoned arrows

Hung on his shoulders,

With pig bladders full of poisoned blood

Fastened close to his chest,

Jiabu said goodbye to his aunt and mounted the winged horse,

Then rushed towards the black horizon.

Jiabu found the monster in the mountain,

And a life-and-death fight started between them.

The monster's sharp horn was aimed at Jiabu,

But the winged horse ducked behind it.

Jiabu's revenging knife

Cut off trees around.

The monster's hard uni-horn

Overturned huge stones nearby.

Jiabu charged forward three times,

And fought backward three times.

The more Jiabu fought, the stronger he became,

while the monster became more ferocious.

Fighting from sunrise,

战到月亮西沉,
甲布和怪兽之间,
三天三夜胜负难分。

甲布愤怒的毒箭,
不能把九层兽皮射穿;
甲布锋利的宝刀,
难得把九双兽脚砍断。

刀箭难把怪物斗倒,
甲布解下备好的猪尿泡,
拴在天马的尾巴下面,
假装战败往后逃。

怪兽趁势追甲布,
独角猛顶马屁股,
猪尿泡被兽角顶破,
鲜红的毒血往外喷出。

怪兽见鲜血满地流,
摇头摆尾笑开口:
"父亲早已变成我角下鬼,
今天儿子又是我嘴边肉。"

Till the moon setting in the west,
Neither Jiabu nor the monster
Could defeat each other in three days and three nights.

Jiabu's poisoned arrows
Could not penetrate the monster's nine layers of skin;
Jiabu's sharp precious knife
Could not cut off the monster's nine pairs of feet.

Seeing that his knife and arrows could not kill the monster,
Jiabu untied the pig bladders,
And fastened them under the tail of the winged horse.
He then pretended to be defeated and began to flee.

The monster took the chance and began chasing Jiabu.
Its horn thrust at the winged horse's bottom,
Broke the pig urinary bladders,
And red poisoned blood gushed out.

When the monster saw the running blood,
Shaking its head and tail, it opened its mouth:
"I killed your father long ago,
And today you will become my food."

支萨·甲布 // Zhisa Jiabu

怪物讲完话，
低头把毒血舔。
甲布拉弩又搭箭，
射向怪物的黑心肝。

怪物中毒又中箭，
狂吼一声往下倒。
庞大的身躯滚下山，
震得山崩地也摇。

甲布已把怪物除掉，
骑着天马往回奔跑。
猛然想起去世的父亲，
调头要把父亲的根骨寻找。

天马拴在小柏树上，
一只黄蜂嗡嗡飞舞，
缠绕天马不愿飞开，
惊马挣扎着拔起了柏树。

甲布牵住天马，
看见柏树已被拔起。
他扒开泥土仔细察看，
父亲的遗骨就在土里。

After saying that,

The monster lowered its head to lick the poisoned blood.

Pulling the crossbow and mounting an arrow,

Jiabu shot at the heart of the monster.

Poisoned by the blood and shot by the arrow,

The monster roared and fell on the ground.

Its huge body rolled down the mountain,

Causing a landslide and the mountain to shake.

Having got rid of the monster,

Jiabu rode the winged horse back home.

He suddenly remembered his deceased dad,

And returned to find his remains.

The winged horse was fastened to a small cypress tree.

A buzzing wasp flew around the horse and the tree.

Disturbing the horse and unwilling to fly away,

Until it scared the horse to pull out the cypress tree.

Jiabu held the horse,

And saw the pulled-out cypress tree.

He dug out some soil to see,

And found his father's remains buried beneath the tree.

小柏树生在父亲的心房,
杨花树长在父亲的头顶上,
小青松紧挨着父亲的手脚,
一朵鲜花在父亲嘴里吐香。

甲布拣回父亲的遗骨,
举行了隆重的葬礼。
普米人送葬要用松、柏、杨树和鲜花,
根子就出在这里。

The cypress tree grew from his heart;

A poplar tree grew from his forehead;

Small pine trees were close to his hands and feet;

A fragrant flower was blooming in his mouth.

Jiabu brought back his father's remains,

And held a grand funeral for him.

The Pumi's use of cypress, poplar, pine trees and flowers at funerals

Originated from this.

第六章

甲布除掉了怪物,
甲布找到了父亲的根骨。
他还要杀死魔王救母亲,
让人间永享太平幸福。

嬢嬢知道甲布的仇恨,
嬢嬢理解甲布的心愿,
她担心甲布的命运,
好心好意把甲布规劝:

"魔王神通广大,
魔王法力无边。
斗魔困难重重,
进山处处艰险。

"生母在魔窟受熬煎,
甲布怎能不去管?
魔法和艰难我不怕,

Canto 6

Jiabu had wiped out the monster;

Jiabu had found his father's remains.

He wanted to kill the Demon and save his mother,

So that people could enjoy eternal peace and happiness.

His aunt knew his hatred,

And understood his wishes.

But she was worried about Jiabu's safety,

And she tried to dissuade him:

"The Demon's power is boundless;

The Demon' magic is endless.

It is extremely difficult to fight against the Demon;

Hardship is everywhere when you go to the mountains."

"My mother is suffering in the Demon's cave.

How could I ignore that?

Magic and hardship I do not fear;

不除魔王誓不生还！"

仇恨能变成聪明和智慧，
愤怒会爆发强力和勇敢。
甲布背上闪亮的箭筒，
挎上牛角做的弩弓，
带上母亲留下的银手镯，
告别嬢嬢把路上。

甲布来到高山巅，
对着东方高声喊：
"打宗里呼哦休休！"
天马随风声出现。

甲布骑上天马，
飞向遥远的天边……

甲布来到一座山前，
刺蓬长满路两边。
刺勾刺，藤缠藤，
横在路心扭作一团。

怎样才能越过刺蓬，
甲布的主意已在心间：

Without killing the Demon I will never come back!"

Hatred can change into intelligence and wisdom;
Rage can lead to strength and bravery.
With shining quiver on his back,
With a bull-horn crossbow hung on his shoulder,
Bringing his mother's silver bracelet with him,
Jiabu said goodbye to his aunt and began his journey.

Jiabu came to the mountain top,
And shouted towards the east:
"Da-zong-li-hu-e-xiu-xiu!"
The winged horse appeared with the wind.

Jiabu mounted the horse,
And flew towards the faraway horizon …

Jiabu came to a mountain,
Where thorns were blocking the way.
Prickles were tied with prickles and vines were entwined with vines,
Forming a huge mess in the way.

How to get away from the thorns?
Jiabu came up with an idea:

"刺蓬，你们的游戏好玩，
能不能让我仔细看一看？"

刺蓬刚停止打架，
甲布纵马跃向前。

甲布走到大河边，
正想催马扬鞭飞对岸，
突然间水咬水怒涛翻卷，
把甲布隔在岸边。

甲布恭敬地对河水道：
"河水，你们的舞姿美妙，
假若能让我学一学，
我愿做你们的奴仆！"

河水停止撕咬分开道，
甲布跃马往前跑。

甲布走到悬崖前，
两座石岩相碰撞，
响声如雷冒火花，
整个大地在摇晃。

"Thorns, your game is really fun.
Could I have a careful look?"

Just when the thorns stopped fighting,
Jiabu rushed his horse to leap over and disappeared.

Jiabu reached a river.
Just before he rushed the horse to fly to the other side,
Suddenly waves rolled high, one after another,
Which stopped Jiabu at the bank.

Jiabu respectfully said to the river,
"River, your dance is graceful.
If you could teach me,
I'm willing to be your servant!"

Just when waves stopped fighting,
Jiabu's horse jumped over the river and ran forward.

Jiabu came to a cliff,
Where two huge stones were colliding with each other,
Causing thunder-like sounds and sparkles,
And the ground to shake.

甲布对着石岩高声喊：
"威武的石岩，巍峨的山，
你们的拥抱真热火，
你们亲嘴真好看。
我向你们道喜，
我向你们问安。"

石岩听到称赞，
各自站立两边。
甲布挥鞭跃马，
飞快跃过石岩。

甲布骑着天马，
像彩云在空中飘荡，
飞过九十九座山岭，
跨过九十九条大江。

甲布骑着天马，
像山鹰在蓝天飞翔，
越过九十九堵悬崖，
腾过九十九块草场。

走了三天又三夜，
跑了三夜又三天，

Jiabu shouted at the stones:

"Grand stones and spectacular mountain,

Your embrace is really hot,

And your kiss is beautiful.

I extend my congratulations to you,

And I am saying hello to you."

Hearing the praise,

The stones stood at both sides of the road.

Jiabu wielded his whip to rush his horse,

And the horse jumped over the stones and cliff swiftly.

Like colorful clouds in the sky,

Jiabu and the winged horse

Flew over ninety-nine mountains,

And crossed ninety-nine rivers.

Like eagles soaring in the blue sky,

Jiabu and the winged horse

Leaped over ninety-nine cliffs,

And passed ninety-nine grasslands.

After riding for three days and three nights,

After running for three nights and three days,

来到一个巨大的山洞口，
洞前流淌着一股清泉。

一路奔波饥渴难忍，
手捧泉水正想饱饮一场，
忽听有人把话讲，
身边出现一个背水的姑娘：

"沟里流的不是水，
沟里淌的是血浆。
劝你莫把人血当泉水，
请你赶快离开这地方。"

甲布听了姑娘的话，
又是愤怒又迷惘：
"好心的姑娘，请你告诉我，
这里是不是魔王住的地方？
我是普米英雄支萨的后代，
我要除掉吃人的魔王。"

"勇敢的普米小伙哟，
你虽是人间英雄的后代。
可这里的天地没有光明，
这里的魔王十分厉害。

He came to the entrance of a big cave,

In front of which flowed a spring.

Hungry and thirsty after a long journey,

He cupped some water and was just about to drink,

When he suddenly heard someone speaking to him,

And beside him appeared a girl carrying a water bucket on her back:

"What flows in the ditch is not water;

What flows in the ditch is plasma.

I advise you not to drink blood as water,

And please leave here as soon as possible."

Hearing what the girl said,

Jiabu became angry and confused:

"Kindhearted girl, please tell me,

Is this the place where the Demon lives?

I am the Pumi hero Zhisa's son,

And I come here to wipe out the man-eating Demon."

"Brave Pumi young man,

Though you are a human hero's son,

Bright prospect here has gone,

Because the Demon here is very powerful."

"洞里人骨堆成山,
洞里人血流满地。
魔王的威力难抗拒,
莫让你的血流进这沟里。"

姑娘说完话,
甲布知内情。
他把手镯放进姑娘的水桶,
给阿妈带个无声的信。

姑娘背水回到山洞,
手镯随水掉进水缸。
响声触动了娜姆的心:
"是不是甲布来到身旁?"

子女长大了,
母亲认不出模样。
母亲变了样,
儿子认不出亲娘。

甲布走进魔洞,
见一个妇人坐在织布机旁,
织出的麻布黑白各半,

"In the cave human bones are piled like a mountain;

In the cave human blood is everywhere.

The Demon's power is irresistible;

Do not let your blood flow into this ditch."

Hearing what the girl said,

Jiabu came to know the truth.

He placed the bracelet into her water bucket,

To bring a silent message to his mother.

The girl carried the water bucket into the cave;

The bracelet dropped into the tank with water.

The sound stirred up Namu's emotion:

"Is Jiabu coming to me?"

When children grow up,

Their mother may not recognize them.

When a mother's appearance changes,

Her son may not recognize her.

Jiabu went into the Demon's cave,

Seeing a woman sitting beside a loom.

Half of the cloth she weaved was black and half white,

甲布知道她是自己的亲娘。

甲布走到母亲身边，
要把母亲的心试探：
"大妈哟，你织的麻，
为啥黑一半、白一半？"

"洁白的麻布为儿织，
时常把甲布儿思念；
黑色麻布为魔王织，
诅咒那吃人的黑心肝。"

"好心的大妈你停一停，
我的头皮痒得很。
请你帮我找找看，
咯有虱子爬头顶？"

甲布投进母亲的怀抱，
娜姆在甲布头上寻找。
猛见甲布头顶的红痣，
伤心的泪水如泉涌冒。

母亲滚烫的热泪，
滴落在甲布的脖颈。

And Jiabu immediately recognized that she was his mother.

Jiabu walked to his mother's side,
And wanted to test her thought:
"Dear aunt, as for the linen cloth you are weaving,
Why is half of it black and half of it white?"

"White cloth is for my son,
And I often miss Jiabu my son;
Black cloth is for the Demon,
The vicious man-eating one that I curse."

"Kindhearted aunt, please stop a moment.
My scalp itches very much.
Please have a look for me.
Is there a louse on it?"

Jiabu dropped into his mother's arms,
And Namu looked at Jiabu's head.
Seeing one red mole on Jiabu's head,
Sad Namu burst into tears.

The mother's hot tears
Dropped onto Jiabu's neck.

鲜红的痣瘢哟苦涩的泪水，
接通了母子断裂的感情。

柴火散开火塘冷，
母子离别心凄凉；
柴火聚拢火塘暖，
母子团圆心欢畅。
娜姆和甲布细商量，
共谋良策除魔王：

"甲布儿哟，
魔王的威力大无比。
救阿妈你要有勇有谋，
除魔王你要胆大心细。
斗魔王要击中要害，
杀魔王要等待时机。

"洞口魔树是魔王的替身，
砍倒魔树魔王就会得病。
魔王的胸前，
有块护心镜，
镜中心有只黄蜂，
那就是魔王的命根。
只要将这只黄蜂射死，

Red mole and sad tears

Repaired the broken affection between the mother and the son.

When firewood is scattered, the fireplace is not warm;

When mother and son are scattered, they become sad.

When firewood is gathered, the fireplace becomes warm;

When mother and son reunite, they become very glad.

Namu and Jiabu discussed carefully,

Trying to find good ideas to kill the Demon:

"Jiabu, my dear son,

The Demon's power is great.

To save your mom you have to be prudent and courageous;

To kill the Demon you must be bold and cautious;

To fight against the Demon you must aim at its crucial point;

To kill the Demon you have to wait for an opportunity. "

"The magic tree at the entrance of the cave is his substitute.

Cut down the magic tree and the Demon will be sick.

On the chest of the Demon,

There is a breastplate.

In the center of the breastplate there is a wasp,

Which is the most important part for the Demon.

If the wasp is shot to death,

魔王就会丧命。

"傍晚你躲在水缸下面，
听到魔王熟睡的鼾声，
用神箭把黄蜂射死，
用神箭射穿魔王的心。"

甲布依照母亲的指点，
来到洞前把魔树砍，
砍开左边，右面又合拢，
砍开右边，左面又还原。

甲布的力气快用尽，
母亲在一旁心中急，
慌忙中想出好主意，
回洞里拿来破褶裙。
褶裙塞进砍口里，
砍开的树口不能重生。

砍到黄昏太阳落，
树干倒地离了根。
魔王身在九山外，
顿时只觉浑身疼。

The Demon will die."

"At dusk you can hide beneath the tank.
When you hear the Demon snoring,
Use your arrows to shoot the wasp to death;
And use your arrows to shoot through the heart of the Demon."

With his mother's direction,
Jiabu came out of the cave to cut the magic tree.
When he cut the left side, the right side healed;
When he cut the right side, the left side recovered.

Jiabu's strength was running out,
And his mother became worried.
In haste she came up with a good idea.
She went to the cave and fetched a torn pleated skirt.
When the skirt was inserted into the cut opening,
The magic tree could not recover again.

Jiabu cut till sunset and dusk,
When the trunk fell on the ground and was disconnected from its roots.
Nine mountains away,
The Demon suddenly felt pain in his whole body.

甲布母子细商量，
魔洞内挖坑巧藏身。
手握弩箭眼不眨，
等候时机杀仇人。

坑口罩上竹筛子，
筛子上架铁三角，
铁三角上放水缸，
魔王卜卦也难找着。

魔王的声音越来越近，
魔王的脚步越听越明。
他念着咒语进山洞，
要把魔殿细搜寻。

往日咒语显神通，
魔殿九次分开又合拢。
今天魔王念咒语，
连念九次魔殿一动不会动。

"可恶的女人你听清，
我要打卦算气运。
快撮来一碗苞谷，
只许一次就撮成。

Jiabu discussed with his mother in detail,

And dug a hole in the cave for hiding.

He had his crossbow and arrows in his hand,

Waiting for an opportunity to kill the enemy.

A sieve was put over the hole;

An iron tripod was put on the sieve;

Then the water tank was put on the iron tripod.

The Demon could not find him even with divination.

The Demon's voice was closer;

The Demon's footsteps were clearer.

He came into the cave chanting spells;

He would search through the cave carefully.

His spells used to be very effective,

And his magic palace divided and reunited nine times.

Today the Demon also chanted the same spells,

But the palace did not move even after he chanted nine times.

"Repulsive woman, listen carefully.

I will divine to tell my fortune.

Scoop up one bowl of corn for me,

And you must succeed with one attempt.

再舀清水一大碗,
不要弄脏不要搅浑。"

娜姆撮苞谷撮了三次,
娜姆舀缸水把水搅浑,
裙子下面绕三次,
脚跨三回落灰尘。

魔王打卦又念咒,
心慌意乱身不安:
"今天的卦象怪得很,
说它不灵又像灵。
今天可能遭厄运,
洞里好像有生人。

"我早就听说支萨有后代,
我早就听说你儿像只虎,
莫非今天仇人进山洞,
莫非支萨的后代来报复?
哼!他要杀我杀不死,
我要喝他的血嚼他的骨。"

魔王说完倒在石床上,
一伙小魔抱来几根木棒。

Then ladle a big bowl of clear water for me,
And you mustn't get it dirty or muddy."

Namu scooped up the corn with three attempts;
Namu ladled water and made it muddy.
She passed it under her skirt three times,
And crossed over it three times to have dirt into it.

The Demon divined and chanted spells,
But became more worried and uneasy:
"Today's divination is quite odd.
It seems ineffective and effective as well.
I may have misfortune today;
There may be a stranger in this cave.

"I heard long ago that Zhisa had an offspring;
I've heard that Zhisa's son is like a tiger.
Could it be that the enemy has come into this cave today?
Could it be that Zhisa's son is coming for revenge?
Hmm! He can never kill me even if he wants to.
I will drink his blood and chew his bones instead."

After that the Demon fell on his stone bed,
And some junior devils brought several wooden poles.

魔王张开血盆大口，
小魔为大王掏牙抓痒。
牙缝里撬出残肉碎骨，
牙缝里流出腥臭的血浆。

坑内的甲布看得分明，
仇恨的怒火冲向脑门。
甲布等魔王睡熟，
张弓搭箭射仇人。

随着"当"的一声巨响，
魔王已被惊醒：
"你这讨厌的女人，
这是什么声音？"

在一旁烤酒的娜姆，
不慌不忙地回答说：
"大王，是我手上的银镯，
碰响了煮酒的铜锅。"

"坏女人，你再敲一下，
看你咯是在骗我。"
娜姆用手镯敲响铜锅，
魔王才放心睡着。

The Demon opened its big mouth

For junior devils to pick teeth and scratch itch for him.

Meat and bone pieces were picked out from between his teeth;

Foul blood flowed out from between his teeth.

Jiabu saw that clearly in the hole;

His hatred rose in his soul.

When the Demon fell asleep,

Jiabu shot an arrow at the enemy.

With a huge "bang",

The Demon was awakened.

"You disgusting woman,

Where does the sound come from?"

Making wine nearby,

Namu replied calmly:

"My king, my silver bracelet

Struck the copper pot which is used for making wine."

"You bad woman, now strike it again

To see if you are cheating."

Namu struck the copper pot with her bracelet,

And the Demon fell asleep in calm.

看准魔王胸前的黄蜂,
甲布射出挖心的神箭。
黄蜂被神箭射死,
魔王的生命死了一半。

甲布对准魔王的心坎,
射出会喝血的神箭,
魔王的心血喷出,
山洞在惨叫声中抖颤。

甲布跳出土坑,
飞身扑向魔王,
双手卡住魔王的脖颈,
仇人间展开了最后的较量。

魔王余力大,
甲布被推翻。
娜姆对准魔王双眼,
撒出一把豌豆面。
甲布趁机掀翻魔王,
双手捏住魔王的命管。
"我的母亲咯是你抢来?
今天不是你死就是我亡!"

Aiming at the wasp on the chest of the Demon,
Jiabu shot his killing arrow.
The wasp was killed by the arrow,
And half of the Demon's life was gone.

Aiming at the Demon's heart,
Jiabu shot another arrow that could drink blood.
Blood burst out from the Demon's heart;
The cave shook due to his painful shouts.

Jiabu jumped out of the hole,
And flew at the Demon.
His hands held the Demon's neck,
And two enemies had a final fight.

The Demon's remaining power was still great,
And Jiabu was pushed down on the ground by him.
Aiming at the Demon's eyes,
Namu threw a handful of pea powder.
Jiabu seized the chance and threw the Demon down,
Seizing the Demon's throat with his hands.
"Did you kidnap my mother?
Either you or I have to die today!"

支萨·甲布 // Zhisa Jiabu

"你的母亲是我抢,
我向你告罪投降。
死前我有三句话,
求你准我讲一讲。"

甲布将手松三下,
魔王垂死做挣扎。
三句咒语念过后,
召来全部兵和马。
要为魔王报仇恨,
要将甲布母子杀。

甲布抽出神马鞭,
朝着魔兵猛抽打。
只听"叭叭"几声巨响,
大小魔兵纷纷倒下。

"你还有什么魔法快使出,
你还有什么诡计快施展。"

"我的气快断,
我的话已完。
最后三口气,

"Your mother was really kidnapped by me.
I am sorry and surrender to thee.
I have three sentences to say before I die;
To express myself today please allow me."

Jiabu relaxed his hands three times,
But the Demon made a last-ditch struggle.
Whispering three spells,
He called in all his devil soldiers.
They wanted to take revenge for the Demon,
And kill Jiabu and his mother.

Jiabu drew out his magic whip;
He beat hard at the devil soldiers.
After several loud crackles,
All the magic soldiers fell on the ground.

" You can play whatever magic you have;
You can play whatever tricks you have."

"My strength has run out;
My words have finished.
Allow me to have three more breaths

让我喘一喘。"

甲布又松了三次手，
魔王吐出毒气三口。
第一口毒气变成跳蚤虱子，
第二口毒气变成蚊子苍蝇，
第三口毒气变成蚂蟥毒蛇，
害虫都是魔王的气血变成。

魔王气断命已亡，
甲布母子喜若狂。
暗黑的天地变明亮，
凋萎的山花吐清香。
小溪欢笑流向大海，
小鸟嬉戏自由飞翔……

To have the last break."

Jiabu relaxed his hands three times;
The Demon emitted three poisonous breaths.
The first breath became fleas and lice;
The second breath became became mosquitoes and flies;
The third breath became leeches and poisonous snakes.
All the pests came from the Demon's breath and blood.

Seeing the Demon had stopped breathing and died,
Jiabu and his mom became wild with joy.
The world became bright and clear;
Withered wild flowers became fragrant.
Joyful springs flowed to the sea;
Birds played and flew freely ...

尾 歌

像星星在晚空闪亮，
像太阳在白天发光；
像高山松柏四季吐翠，
像江河流水万年流淌。
普米的英雄支萨·甲布，
为民除害人人敬仰；
普米的儿子支萨·甲布，
英雄的事迹代代传扬！

Epilogue

Like stars twinkling in the sky,

Like the sun shining in the daytime,

Like mountain pine and cypress trees evergreen in all seasons,

Like rivers flowing for endless time,

The Pumi hero Zhisa Jiabu

Is respected by everyone for wiping out disasters;

The heroic deeds of Zhisa Jiabu, the Pumi's son,

Are spread throughout every generation.

支萨·甲布 // Zhisa Jiabu

About the Translator

Liu Dezhou is a professor of English in the School of Foreign Languages and Literature at Yunnan Normal University. His recent publications include two monographs, *Studies and Practice of Reflexology* and *A Contrastive Study of Tautology in English and Chinese* and several articles in academic journals. He also participated in the translation or editing of several books and textbooks. Professor Liu is an experienced simultaneous interpreter and he has interpreted in over 200 international forums, workshops and seminars for many international organizations and Chinese ministries, departments and organizations in his spare time.

云南新华一厂
检验员
04